HELPING YOUR BRAND-NEW READER

Here's how to make first-time reading easy and fun:

▶ Read the introduction at the beginning of the book aloud. Look through the pictures together so that your child can see what happens in the story before reading the words.

▶ Read the first page to your child, placing your finger under each word.

▶ Let your child touch the words and read the rest of the story. Give him or her time to figure out each new word.

▶ If your child gets stuck on a word, you might say, *"Try something. Look at the picture. What would make sense?"*

▶ If your child is still stuck, supply the right word. This will allow him or her to continue to read and enjoy the story. You might say, *"Could this word be 'ball'?"*

▶ Always praise your child. Praise what he or she reads correctly, and praise good tries too.

▶ Give your child lots of chances to read the story again and again. The more your child reads, the more confident he or she will become.

▶ Have fun!

First edition 2000

Library of Congress Cataloging-in-Publication Data
Friend, Catherine.
Funny Ruby / Catherine Friend ; illustrated by Rachel Merriman—1st ed.
p.   cm. — (Brand new readers)
Summary: Four stories about the antics of a silly sheep named Ruby
as she picks flowers, jumps, eats hay, and plays with a friend.
ISBN 0-7636-1066-6
[1. Sheep—Fiction.] I. Merriman, Rachel, ill. II. Title. III. Series.
PZ7.F91523   Fu 2000
[E]—dc21   00-028946

2 4 6 8 10 9 7 5 3 1

Printed in Hong Kong

This book was typeset in Letraset Arta.
The illustrations were done in watercolor, gouache,
and colored pencil.

Candlewick Press
2067 Massachusetts Avenue
Cambridge, Massachusetts 02140

FUNNY RUBY

CANDLEWICK PRESS
CAMBRIDGE, MASSACHUSETTS

Catherine Friend ILLUSTRATED BY **Rachel Merriman**

Contents

Buzz Buzz Buzz   1

Ruby Jumps   11

Ruby Eats Hay   21

YUCK!   31

BUZZ BUZZ BUZZ

1

Introduction

This story is called *Buzz Buzz Buzz*. It's about all the things Ruby the sheep picks from the field and gives to Jane the farmer, including a flower with a bee!

Ruby picks some grass.

Jane takes the grass.

Ruby picks some clover.

6

Jane takes the clover.

Ruby picks a flower.

buzz buzz buzz

8

The flower has a BEE.

Jane sees the bee.

10

Jane runs away.

RUBY JUMPS

11

Introduction

This story is called *Ruby Jumps*.
It's about how Ruby the sheep jumps
all over the farm and what she does
when she jumps on Kate the cow.

Ruby jumps.

14

She jumps over the bush.

She jumps over the log.

16

She jumps over the flowers.

She jumps over the water.

Ruby jumps over Kate.

19

OOPS!

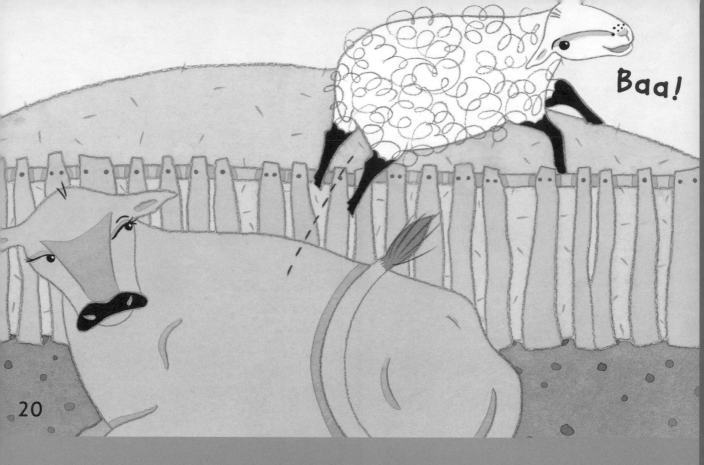

Baa!

Ruby jumps again.

RUBY EATS HAY

Introduction

This story is called *Ruby Eats Hay*.
It's about how Ruby the sheep eats
hay until she disappears under the
pile of hay, and what happens when
Kate the cow eats hay too.

Ruby eats hay.

24

Munch, munch.

Ruby eats more hay.

Munch, munch, munch.

Ruby eats and eats.

Kate sees the hay.

Kate eats hay too. Munch, munch!

30

Kate sees Ruby!

YUCK!

Introduction

This story is called *YUCK!* It's about
how Ruby the sheep smiles when Jane the
farmer pats her, until Ruby gives Jane
a yucky lick on the cheek.

33

Jane pats Ruby's head.

34

Ruby smiles.

Jane pats Ruby's ear.

Ruby smiles.

Jane pats Ruby's nose.

Ruby smiles.

Ruby licks Jane's cheek.

40

"YUCK!" says Jane.